Mel Bay Presents

Steve Kaufman's Favorite 50 Celtic Reels Tunes A-L for Mandolin

CD Contents

1	Ash Plant
2	Big Ship
3	Blackberry Blossom
4	Bonnie Breas Of Skelmorlie
5	Bonnie Kate
6	Bonnie Lad
7	Bonnie Laddie
8	Bonniest Lass in A' the World
9	Boy in the Gap
10	Boys of the Lough
11	Braes of Auchtertyre
12	Bunker Hill
13	Cameronian
14	Cameronian Rant
15	Captain Keller
16	Captain McIntosh
17	Cathal McConnell's
18	Charming Katie
19	Clean Pease Strae
20	Cock Your Pistol, Charlie
21	College Groves
22	Colonel Lennox's Love
23	Connemara Stockings
24	Cork Lasses
25	Dark-Haired Lass
26	Diamond Reel
27	Doctor Gilbert
28	Donalblane
29	Donegal
30	Down the Broom
31	Downshire Reel
32	Drunken Crow
33	Dunkeld Hermitage
34	Fairy Reel
35	Fandango
36	Far from Home
37	Five Mile Chase
38	Flax in Bloom
39	Flora McDonald
40	Flower of the Flock
41	Girl I Left Behind Me
42	Girl With the Blue Dress On
43	Green Groves of Erin
44	Greig's Pipes
45	Grey Daylight
46	Hand Me Down the Tackle
47	Highland Fling
48	Highland Plaid
49	Highlander's Kneebuckle
50	Honourable Miss Buller's
51	Humours of Carrigaholt
52	Humours of Westport
53	I'll Break Your Head for You
54	In the Tap Room
55	Isle of Skye
56	Jack Latten
57	Jackson's Chickens
58	John Stetson's Reel
59	Jolly Tinker
60	King George the Fourth
61	Kiss Me Kate
62	Lady Caroline Birtitle
63	Lady Corbett's Reel
64	Lady Cuffe's Fancy
65	Lady Madelina Sinclair's Reel

1 2 3 4 5 6 7 8 9 0

Visit us on the Web at www.melbay.com — E-mail us at email@melbay.com

Table of Contents

Introduction 04
About the Author 08
Understanding the Tablature....09
Understanding the Timing 13
Suggested Rolls 17

CD Markers **Page Number**
01. Ash Plant....19
02. Big Ship 20
03. Blackberry Blossom 21
04. Bonnie Breas of Skelmorlie 22
05. Bonnie Kate 23
06. Bonnie Lad 24
07. Bonnie Laddie 25
08. Bonniest Lass in A' the World 26
09. Boy in the Gap 27
10. Boys of the Lough 28
11. Braes of Auchtertyre....30
12. Bunker Hill 32
13. Cameronian....34
14. Cameronian Rant 35
15. Captain Keller....36
16. Captain McIntosh 37
17. Cathal McConnell's 38
18. Charming Katie 39
19. Clean Pease Strae 40
20. Cock Your Pistol, Charlie 41
21. College Groves 42
22. Colonel Lennox's Love 44
23. Connemara Stockings....45
24. Cork Lasses 46
25. Dark-Haired Lass 47
26. Diamond Reel....48
27. Doctor Gilbert....49
28. Donalblane 50
29. Donegal....51
30. Down the Broom 52
31. Downshire Reel 53
32. Drunken Crow 54

33. Dunkeld Hermitage 55
34. Fairy Reel 56
35. Fandango 57
36. Far from Home 58
37. Five Mile Chase 59
38. Flax in Bloom 60
39. Flora McDonald 61
40. Flower of the Flock 62
41. Girl I Left Behind Me 63
42. Girl with the Blue Dress On 64
43. Green Groves of Erin 65
44. Greig's Pipes 66
45. Grey Daylight 68
46. Hand Me Down the Tackle 70
47. Highland Fling 72
48. Highland Plaid 73
49. Highlander's Kneebuckle 74
50. Honourable Miss Buller's 75
51. Humours of Carrigaholt 76
52. Humours of Westport 77
53. I'll Break Your Head for You 78
54. In the Tap Room 79
55. Isle of Skye 80
56. Jack Latten 81
57. Jackson's Chickens 82
58. John Stetson's Reel 84
59. Jolly Tinker 85
60. King George the Fourth 86
61. Kiss Me Kate 87
62. Lady Caroline Birtitle 88
63. Lady Corbett's Reel 90
64. Lady Cuffe's Fancy 91
65. Lady Madelina Sinclair's Reel 92

Steve Kaufman's Discography 93

Steve Kaufman's Favorite Fifty Celtic Reels for Mandolin Tunes A-L

Introduction

I have always been into fiddle tunes of any kind. Celtic, Appalachian, Canadian and Texas fiddle tunes have been my forte and main stay of selection because of the intensity and drive found in the tunes and the history behind them. I am very happy to bring this compilation of *Steve Kaufman's Favorite Fifty Reels A-L* to you in a format that should be easy to learn. The title implies 50 but I couldn't hold this collection to just that so I have actually included 66 beautiful Reels that I am sure you will enjoy.

Let me give you a little background on the evolution of this book. It took about one and a half years to complete aided by friends on both sides of the water. I had been playing Celtic tunes all my life so writing a book on the subject seemed at first to be right up my alley and truly a magnificent yet enormous project. I got started in January of 1998 doing the preliminary research and writing out some tunes that I knew but it wasn't until August of 1998 that I got the real feel for the music. My family and I took a 24-day trip touring England, Ireland and Scotland. Meetings were set up through several friends in those countries where some of the finest pickers were assembled and I was able to record them and ask questions. It originally came out as *Kaufman's Encyclopedia of Celtic Fiddle Tunes For Mandolin.* This large book included 275 songs and was quite massive in weight and price. It also did not include any CDs. So Bill Bay and I decided to break the manuscript into four volumes – Hornpipes, Waltzes and Jigs, Reels A- L and Reels L-W. I was also able to record all 275 songs so now all four books are complete with CD.

I came to these afore mentioned sessions prepared with my trusty mini-disc recorder ready to record tunes and conduct interviews. The instruments at these jam sessions were often fiddles, pipers, button accordions, button harmonica, banjos and guitars. The musicians were all incredibly proficient. It gave me a feeling that every picker in the United Kingdom was world-class talent. More often than not, at the end of each inspiring and now recorded tune I would ask "What was that tune called?" and a typical answer would be "It doesn't matter."

It doesn't matter was a phrase I heard very often. And this was a remarkable lesson. I soon learned that it really does not matter what the tunes were called. As explained to me in great detail near the end of my journey for the quest for new and interest traditional Celtic fiddle tunes along with the titles, the tune is the tune. The tune is the important factor and the title is nothing more than something you and I can use to categorize or place the song into a slot of some kind. You use the title to specify and remember certain tunes but the title is the least important part of the tune- it's only a tag or like a post-it note.

I was at a session in Cambridge, England set up by guitarist Mark Jones, at the home of Lucy Delap and Clive Lawson. Lucy and Clive are great fiddlers and to break up the two fiddles, Lucy switches to the pipes. Lucy's sister, Mary Nugent, an incredible wooden flutist and Mark Jones were there too. The session was wonderful. I did not recognize any tunes but the music was strong and seeping with tradition and history. I was taping tunes and gathering information when I was asked to break out the guitar and "trade tunes". I tuned up and was ready to pick the next tune with my hosts when I asked Clive "What's the chords to this one?" and he replied (you guessed it) "It doesn't matter."

This was like the final straw for this formal picker and I argued that you can't play just anything. You need to know the key and then the sub-tones that fit with the notes of the songs making up the chord structure. He then replies in a friendly and unassuming way "it doesn't matter". Then in walks another picker, Andy Locker, and when he breaks out the banjo I asked what the chords were and he looked at me and said as plain as day "it doesn't matter". Clive gave me a look that could cut like a hot knife through blood pudding and I was compelled to then believe him. And through this important lesson, I learned again that "It Doesn't Matter," for Celtic music anyway. Also in this Cambridge session was Hazel Fairbairn on fiddle, Josie Nugent fiddle. I remember a funny story from that session. When I was asked to trade tunes I played one that I had learned while working on my *Kaufman's Collection of American Traditional Fiddle* Tunes For Guitar. We passed it around and Lucy picked right up on it and we played another it another few minutes. Lucy then asked what it was called. I told her that we call it "Green Fields Of America" and she said in the sweetest Irish accent "Oh No...... we call that 'There's A Hole In My Heart Large Enough To Stuff A Turnip In It' (see the song in this book). What a great title. Thank you all for the great session and lesson.

The 'Key' is important to the tune. This tells us if the song "sounds" right when playing the notes in sequence. The chord or background harmony tones will have to match these tones somehow but when you physically attach a solid and defined chord structure to a Celtic tune you have somehow tampered with tradition. These old and traditional tunes had no chords when they were written. They were 'The Tunes'. Any harmonies (chords) only augment the tune but they are not now or ever cast in stone. The chords written in this book are only a small example of what can be done in the background. They are only a suggestion so feel free to use what sounds best to you at the time. I was taught another lesson. Keep in mind that the guitar is somewhat new to this music compared to pipes and fiddles.

I had a great experience taping a bagpipe player in Colander, Scotland. He was a National Champion Piper who was busking at a tourist bus station in order to practice. He said his room mates didn't want to hear him all day long so he goes to the streets and makes a little (a lot of) change at the same time. He regularly performs at Sterling Castle.

A friend of mine in Dublin set up a session that explained a lot to me about Pub Sessions. His name is Ronnie Norton of Norton and Associates in Dublin. Ronnie is a great friend to music and musicians and happens to be (in mine and his countrymen's opinion) one of the greatest photographers in Ireland along with a running brilliant graphic arts business. He set up a pub session for me with several in attendance. I witnessed something all together new to me. We in America play either bluegrass style or Old Timey style. That is to say in bluegrass style everyone playing gets a solo while the rest of the jammers play rhythm or back up. Old Time play is closer to Pub Session Celtic players in that they all play in unison. Everyone plays at the same time, note for note identically so that no one is the star in the light. This is a very strong sounding way of playing music and is very enjoyable to listen to. Most of the time someone calls out a song and the one song is played for 5 minutes or so.

In the Celtic Pub Sessions they play "sets" of songs. This was one of the neatest things I witnessed. The fiddler would mutter something, put the fiddle under his/her chin look up at all the musicians and start a tune. Then after a few rounds of 250 BPM unison play, the fiddler would look up with his eyes only, as if looking over his glasses, and BOOM!, they would be into another song without a word said. Then after two to three rounds of the next tune in unison BOOM!, they would go into another tune. This author did all he could to hold on. They would go through 4 or 5 songs to the set. What a thrill- this is an exciting way to play and to beat all, these musicians were great! They get together one or two times a week at this pub for who knows how many years, and this goes on at almost every pub in the U.K.

Ronnie Norton still speaks the ancient Gaelic language and has helped in the translation of some of the tunes in this book. One in particular is called Muckin' O'Geordie's Byre. I sent Ronnie an E-mail and his reply was swift and true. He said-*"Good to hear from you and to see that the ancient art of slang translation is still of value. As we better spoken folk would say "Muckin' O'Geordie's Byre" is properly pronounced as "The Mucking Out Of Geordie's Byre." In which Byre means cow shed or stable and mucking out refers to an old Irish or British custom of washing and sweeping the floor of said stable after the bovine residents have soiled it. Geordie is the nickname given to a gentleman who hails from the area of England around the river Tyne and towns such as*

Newcastle-upon-Tyne. Muck is a colloquial noun, which broadly refers to any damp or watery dirt such as wet clay, or fresh animal manure so therefore mucking is a verb relating to the cleaning out of the aforementioned substance.

What it really means is "We shoveled the poop out of Geordie's cow house", but don't say that I told you. And if that's not a load of Bull then I don't know !!!!!!" And thank you Ronnie for that definitive response.

I think the two greatest experiences of the trip was getting a glimpses into the lives of the people that live and breath this great art form of music. The friends we met are hard working, honest people with strong a heritage and sense of tradition. I will always look forward to any trip back to this old world of new friends. The second greatest experience was being able to be on this glorious trip with my family. Mark and Donna (my head of Sales and Marketing and my Director/Producer respectively) were there to enjoy the new world. Upon our return to Tennessee I asked Mark what his favorite part of the trip was and he said "staying in the land of the Castles."

Rhythm:

Hornpipes have a loping sound to them so the one measure sweeping strum will sound like DA-da-DA-da DA-da-DA-da with accents on the down beats (the DA's) and a light up strum on the up beats (the da's).

Jigs generally have 6 beats in every measure so the rhythm has to also reflect this. Count over and over - 1, 2, 3, 4, 5, 6, 1, 2, 3, 4, 5, 6, 1, 2, 3, 4, 5, 6 etc. Let's make the strums with the pick hand represented by a "D" for a down strum and an "U" for the up swing. Now count the numbers again and then picture it with the strums going D U D D U D DUDDUD or you could go DxU DUD DxUDUD and yet another pattern could be DxU DxU which is again a loping kind of sound. Another pattern that I saw popular though it is very difficult to get fast is: DDU DDU DDU DDU. Whichever you chose keep in mind that

a) It doesn't matter and

b) Don't add extra beats into the 6 beat measure.

Reels/Rants. A reel is a rant so when you see that in print you'll know what we are talking about. Reels seem to be the fastest of the three main types of Celtic tunes. They would be like the USA's breakdown. These songs are generally played with alternating bass/strum patterns.

Chord Structure:

You will find that some of the chord harmonies differ from the common North American progressions. I found the different chord structures fascinating, logical and very pretty. They were just a little different than the usual I, IV, V progressions I've gotten used to in Appalachian fiddle tunes but they definitely grow on you and can be used in many other types of music.

Feeling the Timing, Lilt and Cadence of the Instrumentals:

The type of tune determines the bounce of the piece. For example the reels are played rather quickly so you won't hear much lilt even though it is there. When played correctly you will hear a long note then short one. The notes are written as straight eighths but they are technically played as a dotted eighth then a sixteenth. They will sound like DA da Da da etc. The faster you play the less gaps you will hear between the notes but the lilt will still be there. When you play the hornpipes you will really feel and hear this dotted note play.

Key Signatures:

The key signature is supposed to reflect the scales and modes used in the song as well as the chord structure of the piece. This is not the case in this book in some instances. In some of the written materials that I used as source, the key signature (number of sharps or flats in the top left corner) did not reflect the actual key of the song. I believe this was done in order to avoid writing in many accidentals (littering the page with many sharps and flats). The key of the song is written as **Key of __**. This is what you should go by.

Tempos and Speeds for Metronome Settings

Here is a guide and starting point to understanding the tempos of the different types of tunes. These are not numbers and tempos that I have come up with in order to frustrate you. They represent the tempo that is comfortable for dancing. See the chart in the **Understanding The Timing** section for further descriptions.

Slip Jigs—a Dotted Quarter Note = 144 bpm

Double Jigs—a Dotted Quarter Note = 126 bpm

Slow Jigs—a Dotted Quarter Note = 80 bpm

Reels—Quarter Note = 225 bpm

Hornpipes—a Quarter Note = 180

In closing this introduction, I want to thank all the people throughout our journeys that helped to bring this project to life. All of our new friends in England, Ireland and Scotland. Those sessions are well etched into my memory and the friends and new faces with be with me always. Special thanks to Mr. William Bay and all the folks behind the scenes at Mel Bay Publications for publishing these works and helping to preserve so much music of all kinds.

I hope you all have a lot of fun and hours of enjoyment playing through these arrangements to some of the finest Celtic tunes that this author is aware of. Keep in mind that there are thousands and thousands of tunes so always be on the look out.

If any (reasonable) questions come up or any comments are to be made please feel free to contact me by either calling 800-FLATPIK (area code + 982-3808) or writing to me at:

PO Box 1020
Alcoa, TN 37701
Steve@flatpik.com or steve@palacetheater.com

Best always

Steve Kaufman

About the Author

Steve Kaufman was born into a musical family in 1957. His father was a jazz piano player and his mother was a classically trained pianist. Music was always around. At four Steve started plinking at the piano and did so for several years. He then moved on to the electric guitar at 10 for a few years and put it away. Next came the cello in 5th grade for a few years. After this Steve picked up the acoustic guitar again and blazed right through a "Folk Guitar" method book. When finished he thought if this is as hard as it gets it's not for him. Then his younger brother, Will, started playing the banjo and his instructor told him he needed a rhythm guitar player to help with his timing. So Steve then picked up his guitar again and got into the bluegrass rhythm. One day Will brought home a Flatt and Scruggs LP, which featured Doc Watson on guitar, and Steve was hooked on flatpicking.

Steve practiced hard with his newfound love of music, sometimes up to 8 hours a day. At age 18 he entered the National Flatpicking Championships in Winfield, KS and made the top 10. The following year was a wash. In 1977, Steve took 2nd place to Mark O'Conner and in 1978, at 21 years old, he returned to win the championship. Then after being barred for 5 years he returned on the 6th year to win the 1984 championships again. Winfield bars the winner for 5 years and they can come back on the 6th year but in 1986 they decided to open up the contest to everyone and not bar the past years champs. Steve returned to win his goal. He became the winner and the first and, at this writing, the only Three Time Winner of the National Flatpicking Championships. He is also noted to have 3 consecutive wins in the Nationals because he was barred all the years he did not enter.

Steve continues to work hard in the world of music. He began producing books and videos in 1989 after teaching private lessons for close to 20 years. His catalog of instructional materials is close to 64 items. His listening CDs and Videos number over 17. Steve began touring the world conducting seminars, workshops, clinics and concerts in 1990 and after 5 years he and his wife, Donna, began "Steve Kaufman's Flatpicking Camp". Every other year they have added more camps into their agenda and now under the title "Steve Kaufman's Acoustic Kamps" they host a Fingerpicking Kamp, Old Time Banjo, Bluegrass Banjo and Mandolin Kamp as well. They have grown into the largest Kamps of their kind in the world with students traveling from around the world to Maryville, Tennessee. In 2002, Steve Kaufman received the Gold Award from a reader's poll in Acoustic Guitar Magazine for running the "Best Workshops, Seminars and Camps."

Steve stays busy being a husband and father, running his Kamps, tour schedule, writing books and recording videos and CDs as well as owning and operating The Palace Theater in downtown Maryville see www.palacetheater.com the areas premier acoustic venue as well as an espresso bar. Also connected to the Palace Theater is a café and deli called the Palace Café and Catering.

Understanding the Notes and Tablature Notes on the Strings

Tablature is one of the fastest systems of learning to play songs that I know. You don't get the benefits of reading notes but you will be up and running quicker. Take time to study the chart of notes and tab above and get familiar with the names of the notes as you are playing them. You will eventually learn the notes on the fingerboard this way. You might even try to study the notes of a song and name the notes using the above chart. Note reading is not difficult. It just takes a little time but when you get it down, you will be able to read music for the mandolin from any source of notes like fiddle, guitar and even saxophone, clarinet and more.

The Tablature system is like a graph or play by numbers method. The **Four Horizontal Lines** represent the strings. The **Top Horizontal Line** represents the first string or the high "E" string. The **Second Horizontal Line** down represents the "A" or the second string. The **Third Horizontal Line** from the top represents the 3rd string or the "D" string and the lowest line represents the fourth or "G" string.

The numbers on the lines represent the frets to be played. A zero "0" on a line is an open string.

Fingering: This is very important to the mandolin pickers. The left hand or fretting hand fingers are 1st, 2nd 3rd and 4th. We don't count the thumb. Use the 1st finger to fret notes found on the 1st and 2nd frets. The 2nd finger frets the 3rd and 4th frets. The 3rd finger frets the 5th and 6th frets and the 4th finger frets the 7th unless otherwise marked.

The numbers that you find in the white area between the notes and the tab are the left hand fingering instructions.

I've written enough notes and hints to get you started with this series and you will pick up more information along your way through this course. Learn to read both the notes and the tablature. If you really want to read the notes, it will come easy to you.

Types of Notes

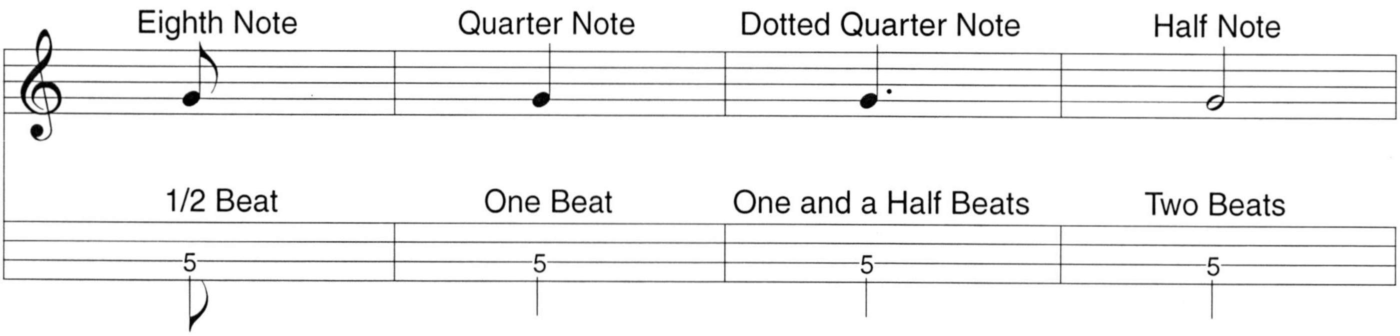

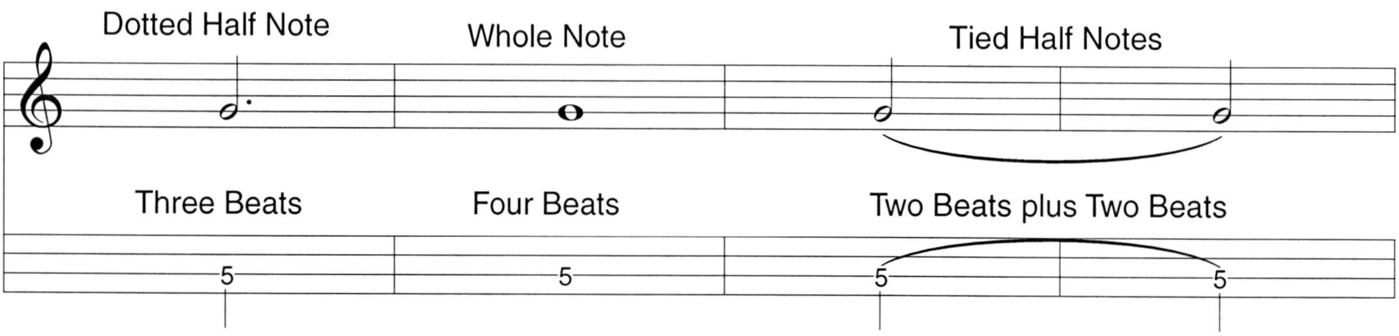

These are all "G" notes. They represent different lengths of time or different amounts of beats.

The first note is an **Eighth Note** (1/8). It is called an eighth note because it would take eight of these notes to make up a whole measure. A measure is bordered by two vertical lines.

Look at the following exercise on page 11. It is made up of eight measures. Count the boxes that are made up of the vertical lines. These are called the "measures". Quarter notes, dotted quarter notes, half notes, whole notes are all hit with down swings. You will find that in my arrangements they almost always fall on the down beat in a measure. Swing down on the down beats and up on the up beats. Every once in a while this doesn't hold true but I will mark the music accordingly and you will also see and understand the change in right hand swings.

Now back to the above chart. An eighth note will last only half of a beat and the way I write tab or notes,when you see an eighth note by itself, it is hit with an up swing and you would go directly to the next note with a down swing.

The next note is a **Quarter Note**. It gets a whole beat and is always hit (99% of the time) with a down swing. Four quarter notes would fill up a whole measure.

Next is a Quarter Note with a dot after it called a **Dotted Quarter Note**. A dot after the note adds half of the value of the note itself. The quarter note gets one beat. Half of that would be a half beat. When you add that back to the original note you get one and a half beats. So the Dotted Quarter Note gets one and a half beats. It is hit with a down swing. When a note like this is present, there is a 99% chance that you will find a single eighth note in the same measure. Pay attention that in the tab you will not see the dot after the number. You will however see a small blank space to the right of the tab note.

The next note is a **Half Note**. It gets two beats. If there were four beats in the measure the half note would take up half the time of that measure. When you see the half note in tablature, it will look like a quarter note. Pay attention to the blank spot to the right of the tab note. Hit the note only one time and let it ring for two full beats. It is hit with a down swing.

Next is a **Dotted Half Note**. It gets three full beats. It is hit with a down swing. Pay attention that in the tab you will only see one note written. Glance up to the notes to confirm the length of time to hold the note.

The next note is a **Whole Note**. It gets four full beats. It is called a Whole Note because it takes up all the beats in the whole measure. It is hit with a down swing. Hit it once and let it ring for 4 full beats. Next to the Whole Note are two **Half Notes tied** together with an arc or a slur. The slur means to combine the total number of beats of the notes involved. How many beats would they last combined?

Note and Tablature Exercises

Exercise One

Play through the following exercise to get familiar with the notes and tablature. Be sure to watch out for the timing. All of the notes are hit with down swings. Play the exercise with the notes first. Check yourself with the notes chart to find where all the notes are, then go through the exercise using the tab. Play it backwards and forwards to help familiarize yourself with the notes and tab. Be sure to play it backwards and forwards.

Trust me - I have my reasons.

Exercise Two

The next few examples deal with timing. The first measure (example one) shows four quarter notes. They are all hit with a down swing. On top of each measure is a row of numbers with an "+" sign between them. When you hit the quarter notes or any notes larger than a single eighth note, they are hit with down swings on the number beats. To see how this works, count out loud 1+2+3+4+. Now hit the notes when you say the numbers. Be sure to count steadily and don't hit any note on an "+" beat. This is the proper way to hit quarter notes.

Example 1

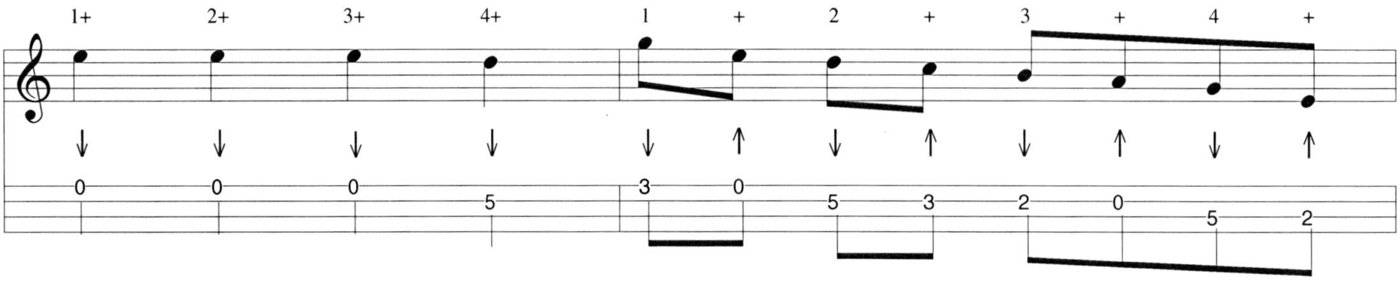

Exercise Three

The next measure (example two) shows eighth notes. It doesn't matter whether the notes are tied or beamed together at the top or the bottom or whether they are grouped in sets of two notes or four notes. The first eighth note is always hit down and the second eighth note is hit up and so on. Count the 1+2+3+4+, hitting the first note down on the number, the second note up on the "+", down on the next number and up on the next "+". Keep it steady. There is very little time between eighth notes. They go as fast as you can count and sometimes faster. Tap your foot while you are counting. Notice that your foot goes down on the numbered beat and up on the "+" beat. Your right hand moves the same way. Practice eighth notes while counting and tapping your foot.

Example 2

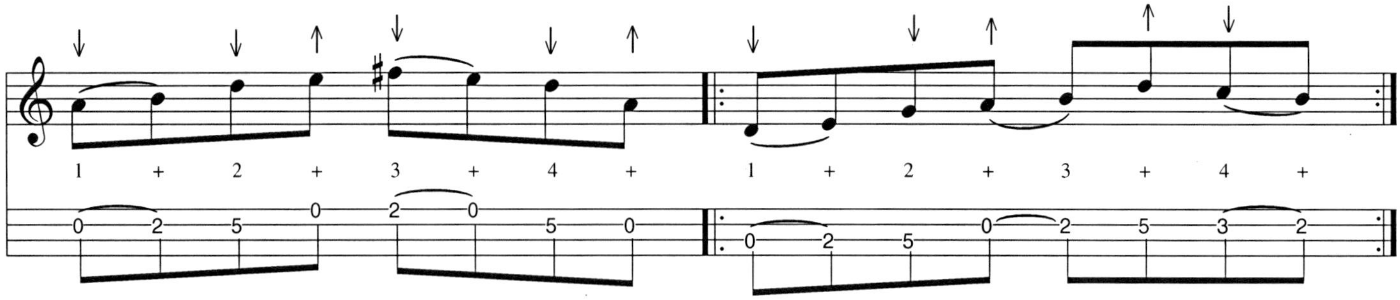

Understanding the Timing

Playing Hornpipes

The timing of hornpipes, even though comprised mostly of eighth notes, is a little different than the reels. Hornpipes are played with the feel of a dotted eighth note followed by a sixteenth note instead of straight eighth notes. The first example of Alexander's Hornpipe is written with the timing denoted how it is to be played. This looks awkward and difficult to read so I wrote the hornpipes in straight eighth note fashion (see the second version or Alexander's Hornpipe) in order to make it a little easier to read.

NOTE: Though written in straight eighth notes be sure to try to capture the dotted eighth and sixteenth note feel.

Alexander's Hornpipe

Example of dotted eighth notes and sixteenth notes

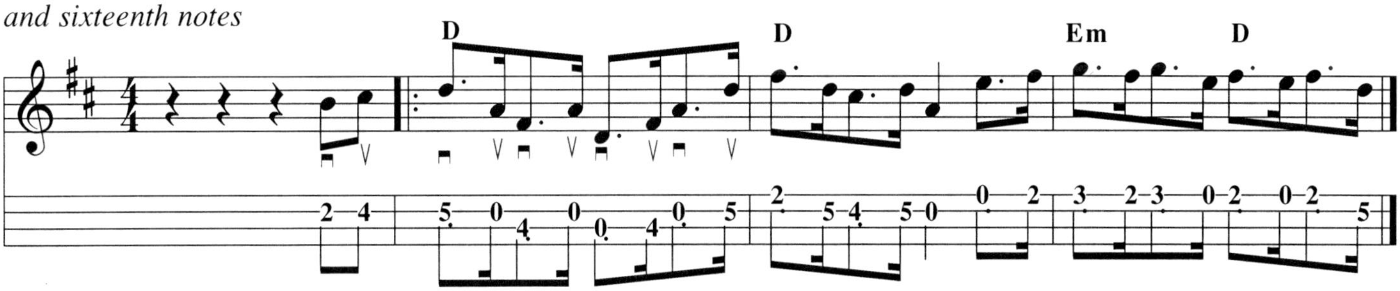

Alexander's Hornpipe

Example of Hornpipes written in this book.:
Straight eighth notes to be played as dotted eighths and sixteenths (see above).

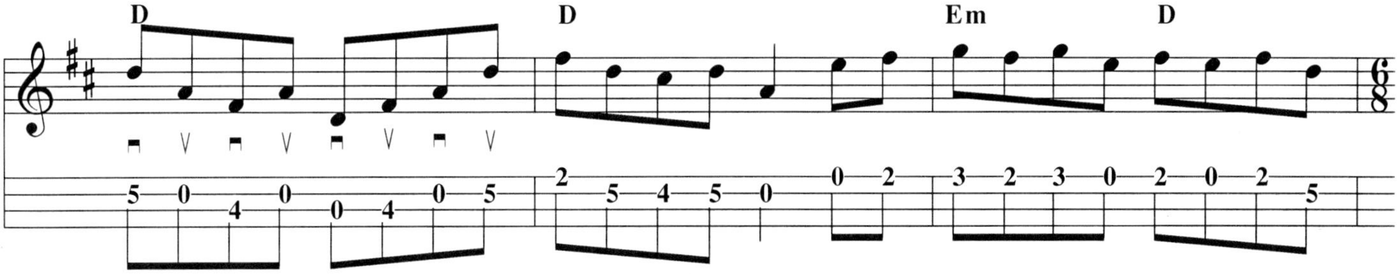

Jigs

Jigs are played differently with the picking hand because the beats are different than those of hornpipes and reels. Jigs are written in 6/8 time which means that there are 6 beats in the measure and the eighth note get a full beat. They play and sound like DA da da DA da da. Usually grouped in two sets three's. Be sure to accent the first note of the three.

Notice the down-up marks in the measures on the next page. You will see some down up down down up down sets and you will see down-up, down-up, down-up sets. You will have to make the call what you do with the right hand. As they say "it doesn't matter" as long as you get the notes in time.

NOTE: Do Not Play Like - down, down, down, down, up, up. This would be incorrect. You will want to get an alternating picking pattern with the picking hand in order to achieve the speed required.

Apples in Winter

Examples of two different picking practices with jigs.

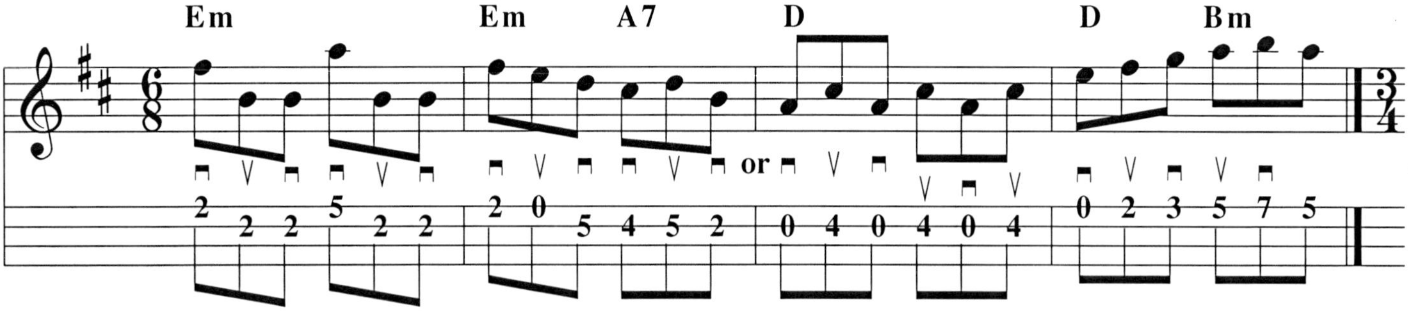

Waltzes

Waltzes comprize some of the most beautiful music written. Unfortunately I could only get a handful in this collection but be looking for more in the future. The waltzes can be pretty plain unless you know a simple way to dress them up. The following two lines illustrate one demonastration.

First learn the tune as written in the book. Then try this. Strum the chord written for the measure from bass to treble to the melody note but not going past the melody note. This technique will accentuate the melody without burying it. If the melody note is note generally found in the chord, you will have to hold the melody note and the remainder of the chord (see the "G" measure in the last line).

Maid of Glenconnel

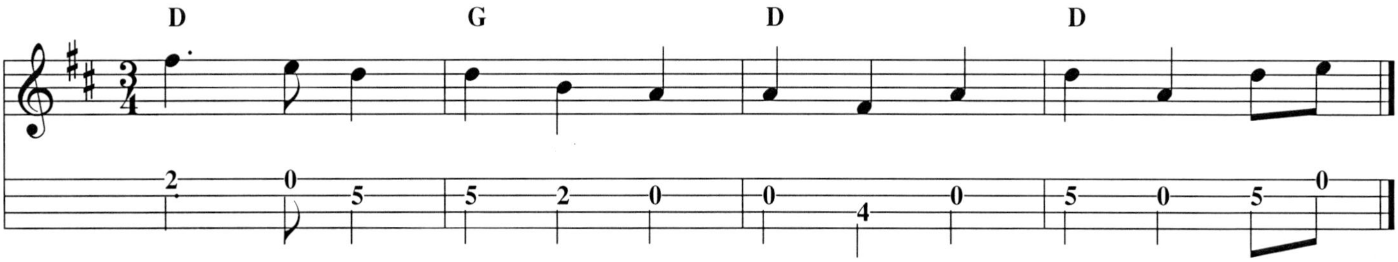

Maid of Glenconnel

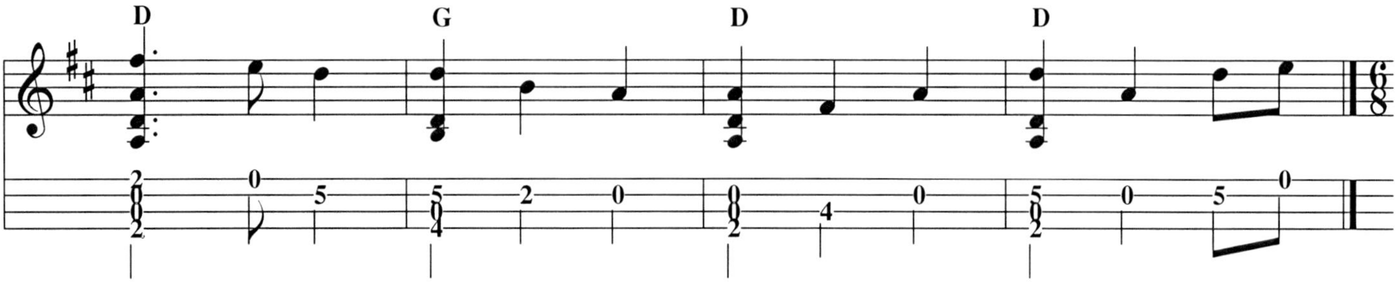

Jigs

There are three variations of the jig: **The Double Jig** in 6/8 time, **The Single Jig** in 6/8 or 12/8 time and the **Hop Jig** - also called a **Slip Jig** in 9/8 time.

The **Double Jig** is delineated from other jigs by its characteristic rhythm of repeated eighth notes:

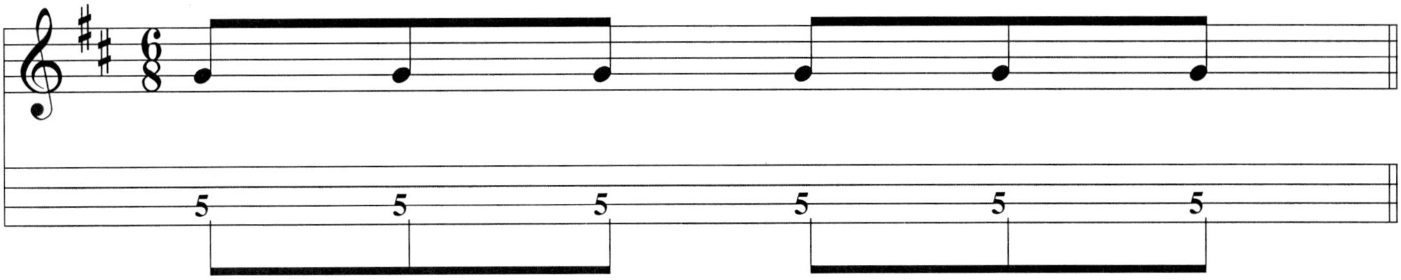

At the player's discretion, repeated eighth notes may also be interpreted with a dotted eighth and sixteenth note rhythm.

The A and B sections of the **Double Jig** will use the running eighth note figure predominantly throughout with the last measure changing to:

The **Single Jig** incorporates more of the Quarter note eighth note combinations

The last bar or measure of a section often ends on a final dotted quater and quater note combination.

The **Slip Jig** of Hop Jig uses various groupings of eighth notes, quater notes and dotted quarter notes.

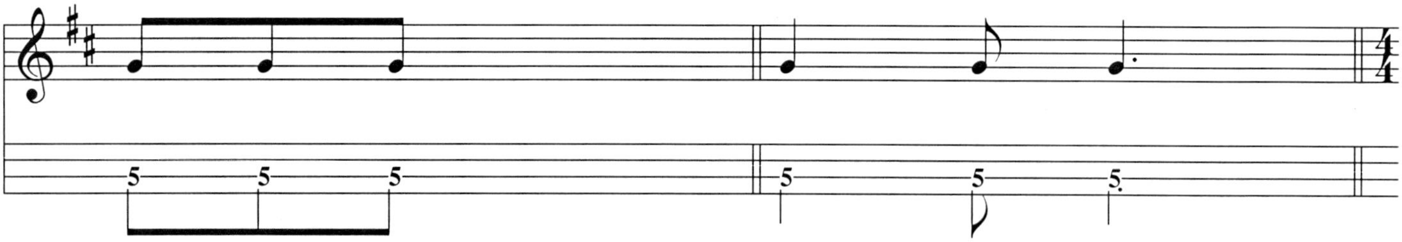

Hornpipes

The Hornpipe is played at a slower tempo than a reel and in a more heavily accented fashion. It is customary for the closing measures of each section in a hornpipe to end with a quarter note set.

The dotted eighth/sixteenth rhythm usually prevails in the performance of the hornpipe. It is frequently notated as a pattern of straight eighth notes. The Hornpipe may also be distinguished by it's formal structure. While it is often a two-part (AB) form, extended forms like ABC, ABCD, AABA etc. may differentiate it from the reel

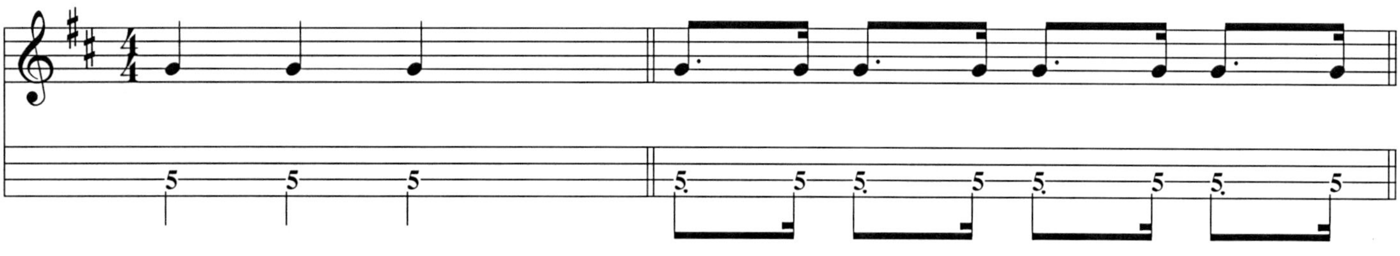

Reels

The **Reel** is the most popular genre of tunes played by traditional instrumentalists. It is often played at a fast tempo, consequently is appeals to the virtuoso player. Strings of repeated eighth notes are often associated with the reel.

Suggested Rolls

Rolls occur when you have a quarter note and you wish to add a bit of flair to the note and song. The first note written in the measures below represent the note to be replaced by the roll. The roll is a five note set of notes that take one beat to execute. In most cases you will hit the first note of the five and then hammer-on, pull-off, hammer-on and then hit the last note on an up swing. Practice these roll/sets until they smooth out. The Celtic fiddles will tell you that you don't really need to hear all of the notes in the roll. It is more a passage of time and a sound that occurs in the music at times when you feel the song needs a little something else. These rolls are often replaced with just a triplet. Practice them and enter them into the songs as desired.

Track #1

The Ash Plant

Key of Em

Arr. by Steve Kaufman

Track #2

The Big Ship

Glise De Sherbrooke

Key of G

Arr. by Steve Kaufman

Track #3

The Blackberry Blossom

The Strawberry Beds

Key of G

Arr. by Steve Kaufman

Track #4

Bonnie Braes of Skelmorlie

Key of D

Arr. by Steve Kaufman

Track #5

Bonnie Kate

Key of D

Arr. by Steve Kaufman

Track #6

The Bonnie Lad

The Bonnie Boy   Because I was a Bonnie Boy

Key of A

Arr. by Steve Kaufman

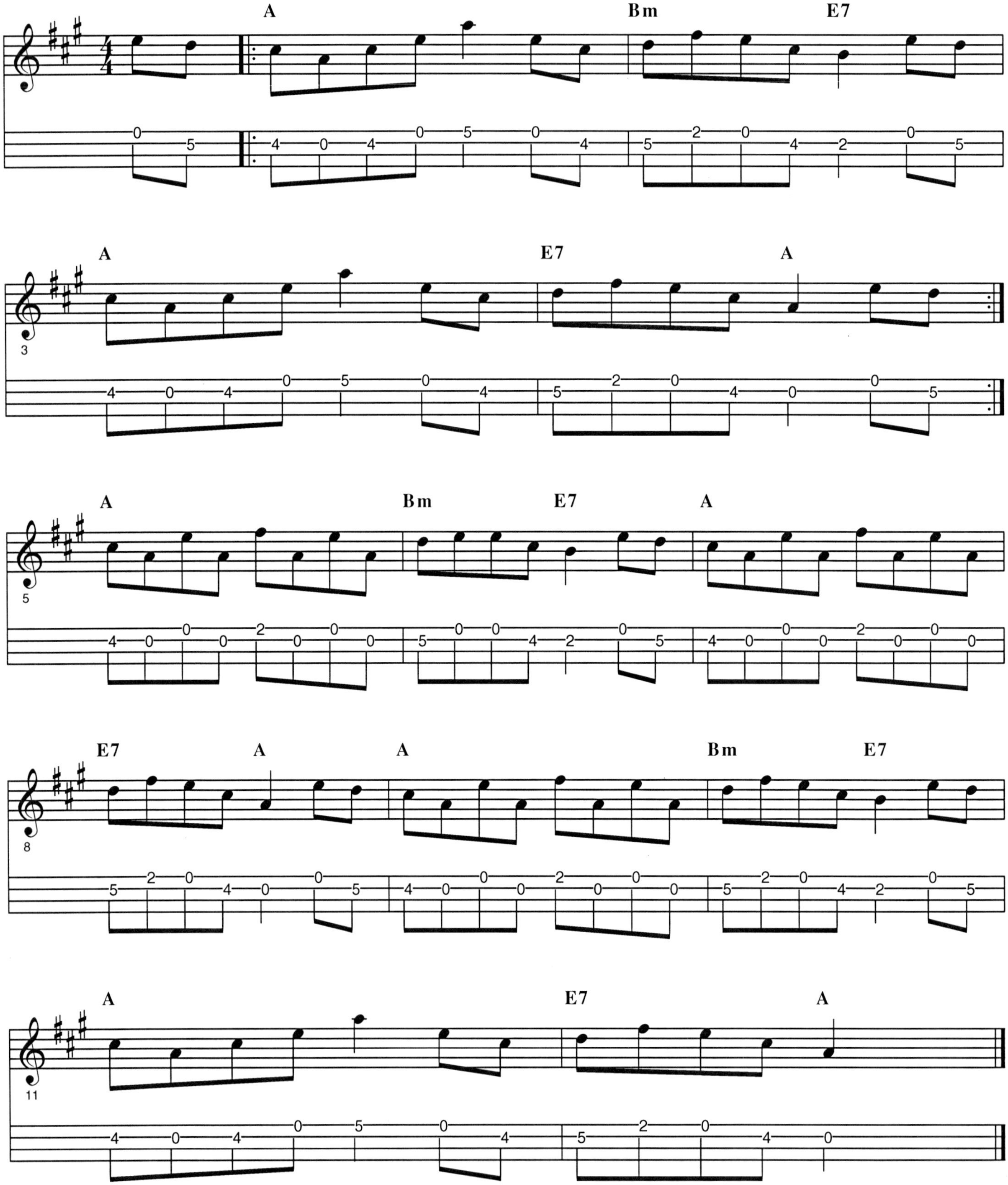

Track #7

Bonnie Laddie

Highland Laddie High Caul'd Cap

Key of G

Arr. by Steve Kaufman

Track #8

The Bonniest Lass in A' the World

The Bonniest Lass in Ayr

Key of A

Arr. by Steve Kaufman

Track
#9

The Boy in the Gap

Key of D

Arr. by Steve Kaufman

Track #10

The Boys of the Lough

Key of D

Arr. by Steve Kaufman

D
A
D
D
A
16
3
Bm
G
D
Bm
C
19
3
D
Bm
G
E7
22
D
A
D
24
3

Track #11

The Braes of Auchtertyre

Key of D

Arr. by Steve Kaufman

Track #12

Bunker Hill

Key of D

Arr. by Steve Kaufman

G C D C D
D D Em
Em D A D C
G C D C D

Track #13

The Cameronian

Carey's Dream Roger's Fancy

Key of D

Arr. by Steve Kaufman

Track #14

The Cameronian Rant

Key of G

Arr. by Steve Kaufman

Track #15

Captain Keller

Key of B♭

Arr. by Steve Kaufman

Track #16

Captain McIntosh

Key of D

Arr. by Steve Kaufman

Track #17

Cathal McConnell's

Key of G

Arr. by Steve Kaufman

Track #18

Charming Katie

Key of A

Arr. by Steve Kaufman

Track
#19

Clean Pease Strae

Key of D

Arr. by Steve Kaufman

Track #20

Cock Your Pistol, Charlie

Captain Murray's Fancy   Gooseberry Blossoms

Key of Am

Arr. by Steve Kaufman

Track #21

College Groves

The Green Jacket

Key of D

Arr. by Steve Kaufman

A
D
C
20
D
A
D
D
23
C
D
A
D
26
C
D
A
D
30

Track #22

Colonel Lennox's Love

Lennox Love to Blantyre

Key of D

Arr. by Steve Kaufman

Track #23

Connemara Stockings

The Galway Reel   Winter Apples

Key of G

Arr. by Steve Kaufman

Track
#24

Cork Lasses

The Sword in Hand

Key of Em

Arr. by Steve Kaufman

Track #25

The Dark-Haired Lass

The Black-Haired Lass

Key of A

Arr. by Steve Kaufman

Track #26

The Diamond Reel

Key of A

Arr. by Steve Kaufman

Track #27

Doctor Gilbert

The Dispute at the Crossroads

Key of Em

Arr. by Steve Kaufman

Track #28

Donalblane

Key of A

Arr. by Steve Kaufman

Track
#29

The Donegal

Key of D

Arr. by Steve Kaufman

Track #30

Down the Broom

Crosses of Annagh

Key of G

Arr. by Steve Kaufman

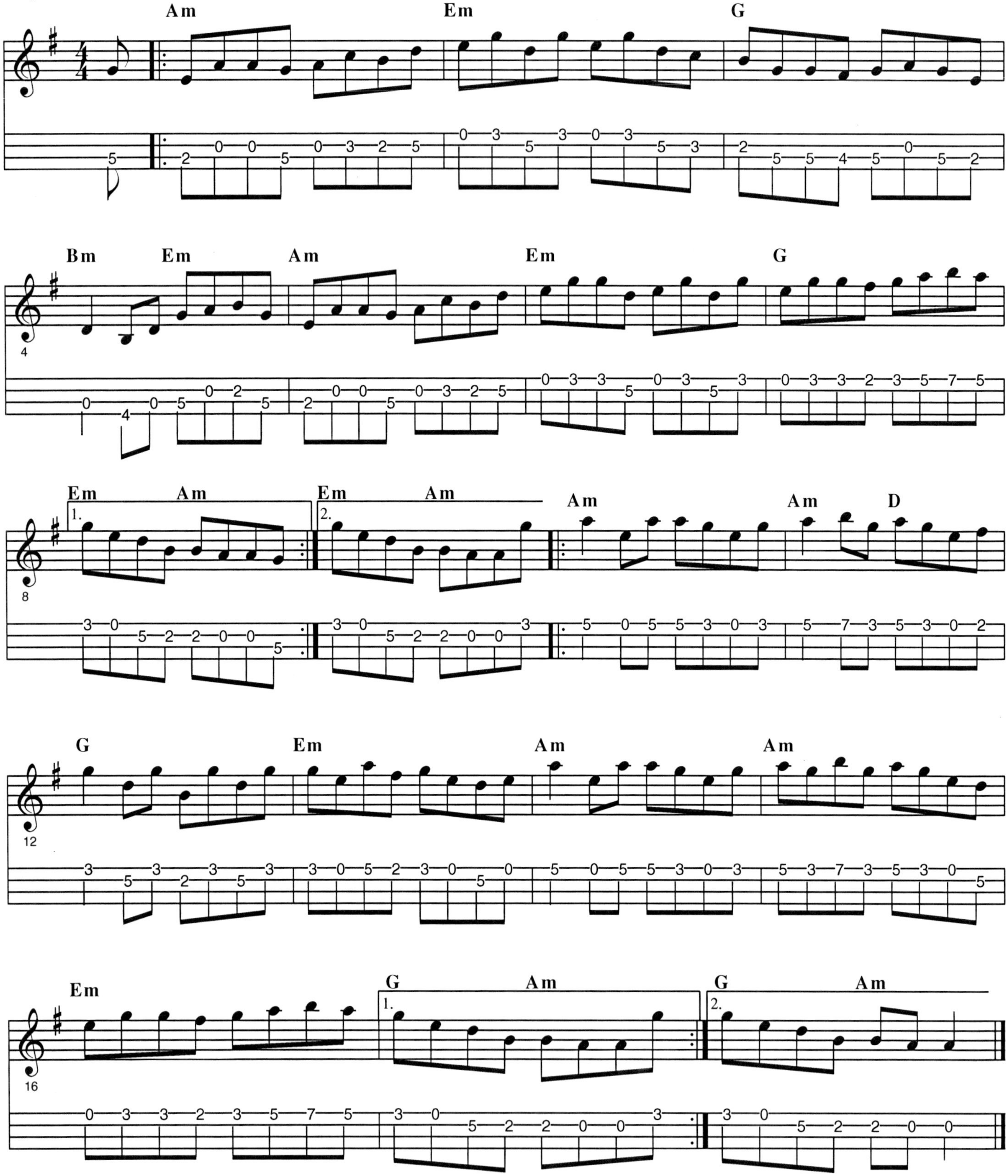

Track #31

The Downshire Reel

Key of Em

Arr. by Steve Kaufman

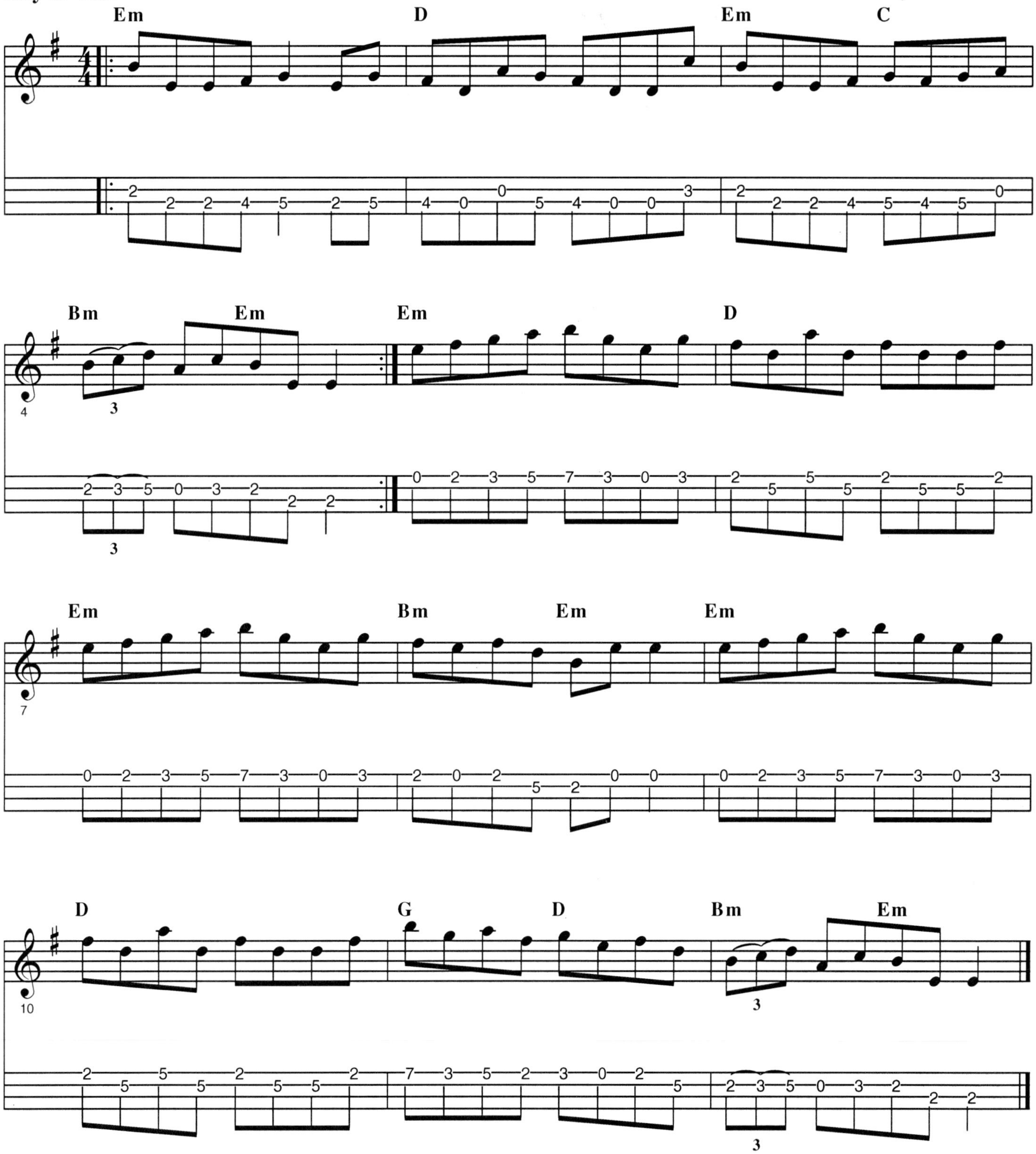

Track #32

The Drunken Crow

Key of G

Arr. by Steve Kaufman

Track #33

The Dunkeld Hermitage

Key of Em

Arr. by Steve Kaufman

Track #34

The Fairy Reel

Haymakers   Old Molly Hare

Key of G

Arr. by Steve Kaufman

Track
#35

Fandango

Key of A

Arr. by Steve Kaufman

Track #36

Far from Home

Key of G

Arr. by Steve Kaufman

Track
#37

The Five Mile Chase

The Yellow-Haired Laddie Corporal Casey's Favorite

Key of G

Arr. by Steve Kaufman

Track #38

The Flax in Bloom

The Lily White

Key of D

Arr. by Steve Kaufman

Track #39

Flora McDonald

Key of Em

Arr. by Steve Kaufman

Track #40

The Flower of the Flock

Key of G

Arr. by Steve Kaufman

Track #41

The Girl I Left Behind Me

Brighton Camp

Key of G

Arr. by Steve Kaufman

Track #42

The Girl with the Blue Dress On

Key of G

Arr. by Steve Kaufman

The Green Groves of Erin

Track #43

Key of D

Arr. by Steve Kaufman

Track #44

Greig's Pipes

Connolly's Reel   The Kerry Huntsman

Key of D

Arr. by Steve Kaufman

D Em D G D
22
G D Bm Em G D
25
G D G D Bm Em
28
G D G D
31

Track #45

Grey Daylight

Stirling Castle

Key of D

Arr. by Steve Kaufman

Track #46

Hand Me Down the Tackle

The Pure Drop

Key of D

Arr. by Steve Kaufman

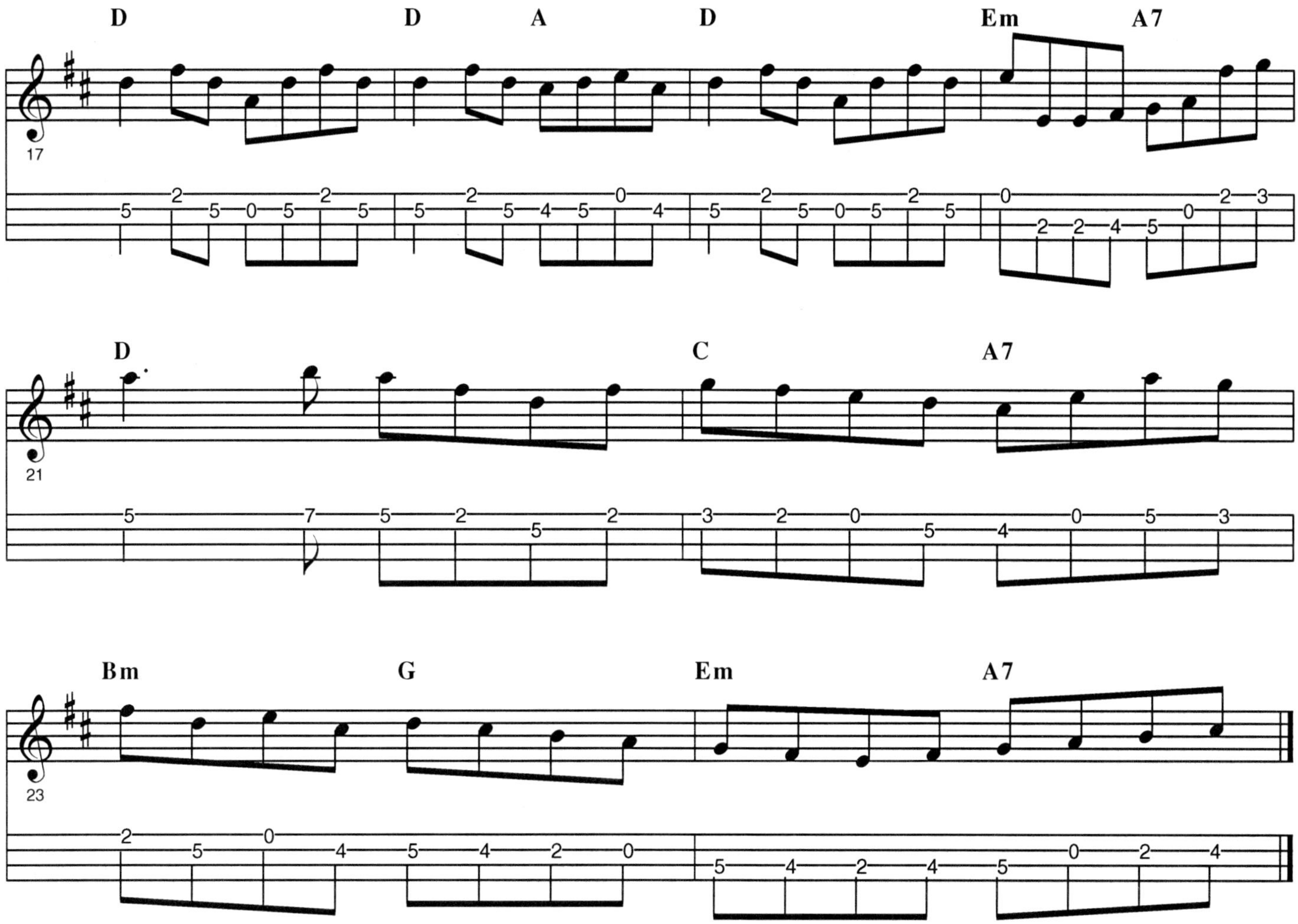
D D A D Em A7
17
D C A7
21
Bm G Em A7
23

Track
#47

The Highland Fling

Miss Drummond of Perth

Key of Am

Arr. by Steve Kaufman

Track #48

The Highland Plaid

Key of G

Arr. by Steve Kaufman

Track #49

The Highlander's Kneebuckle

Leather Buttons

Key of G

Arr. by Steve Kaufman

Track #50

The Honourable Miss Buller's

Key of D

Arr. by Steve Kaufman

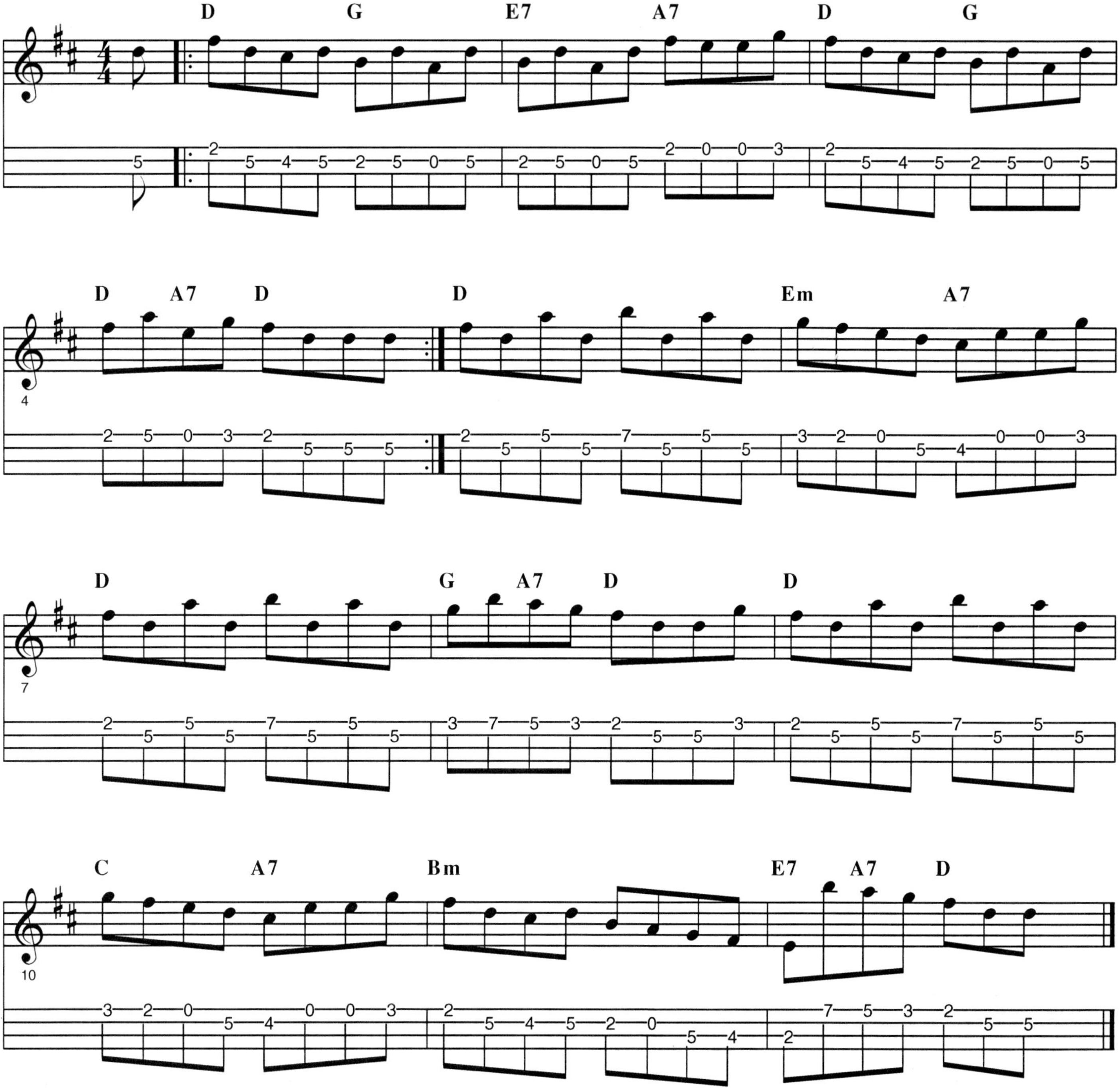

Track #51

The Humours of Carrigaholt

Key of D

Arr. by Steve Kaufman

Track #52

Humours of Westport

Key of F

Arr. by Steve Kaufman

Track #53

I'll Break Your Head for You

Key of B♭

Arr. by Steve Kaufman

Track #54

In the Tap Room

The Blossom of the New Tree, Captain Murray's, Cock Your Pistol Charlie, Granshaw Glens, Hopetown House, The Lady's Top Dress, The Mountain Lark, The Rakes of Abby, The Ranting Widow, Roll Out the Barrel, The Scotch Bonnet, A Short Way to Heaven, The Tap House, The Youngest Daughter

Key of Bm

Arr. by Steve Kaufman

Track #55

Isle of Skye

Key of G

Arr. by Steve Kaufman

Track
#56

Jack Latten

Jennie Rock the Cradle

Key of A

Arr. by Steve Kaufman

Track
#57

Jackson's Chickens

Key of D

Arr. by Steve Kaufman

D G D
A7 D
1.
A7 D
2.
16
D
D G
D
19
D Em
D
D A7
22
D G D
A7 D
1.
A7 D
2.
25

Track #58

John Stetson's Reel

Key of D

Arr. by Steve Kaufman

Track #59

The Jolly Tinker

Key of G

Arr. by Steve Kaufman

Track #60

King George the Fourth

Key of Am

Arr. by Steve Kaufman

Track #61

Kiss Me Kate

Charming Molly's Reel

Key of G

Arr. by Steve Kaufman

Track #62

Lady Caroline Birtitle

Key of D

Arr. by Steve Kaufman

G D A D
15
C
D Em A7 D Em
17
A D D Em A
20
D Em A D
23

Track #63

Lady Corbett's Reel

Key of D

Arr. by Steve Kaufman

Track #64

Lady Cuffe's Fancy

Key of G

Arr. by Steve Kaufman

Track #65

Lady Madelina Sinclair's Reel

Key of G

Arr. by Steve Kaufman

Steve Kaufman's Instructional Materials also at www.flatpik.com

Kaufman's Favorite Fifty Celtic Hornpipes for Flatpicking Guitar Book and CD

Kaufman's Favorite Fifty Celtic Jigs and Waltzes for Flatpicking Guitar Book and CD

Kaufman's Favorite Fifty Celtic Reels A through L for Flatpicking Guitar Book and CD

Kaufman's Favorite Fifty Celtic Reels L through W for Flatpicking Guitar Book and CD

Classic Arrangements to Vintage Songs - Book with 2 CDs

Band in the Book for Bluegrass Vocals - Book with CD

Band in the Book for Bluegrass Instrumentals - Book with CD

Band in the Book for Gospel Vocals - Book with CD

Bullet Train - The Book with Full CD

Kaufman's Collection Of Traditional American Fiddle Tunes Book and 2 CDs

Kaufman's Collection Of Traditional American Fiddle Tunes DVD

Flatpicking The Gospels for Guitar Book with CD and DVD

Flatpicking The Rags and Polkas - Book w/ 2 CDs

Championship Flatpicking Book with CD and DVD

You Can Teach Yourself Flatpicking Guitar with CD or DVD

The Complete Flatpicking Book with CD and DVD

Smokey Mountain Christmas For Guitar - Book with CD

The Power Flatpicking Fingerboard Book with CD and DVD

Blazing Guitar Solos for One or More Book with CD

The Legacy Of Doc Watson - Book

The Anthology of Norman Blake - Book

Flatpicking Banjo Tunes for Guitar - DVD with Booklet

Figuring Out The Fingerboard for Guitar - DVD with Booklet

Learn to Play Waltzes Flatpicking Style - Video with Booklet

4-Hour Celtic Workout Book with 4 CDs

Picking Up Speed - DVD with Booklet - Drills for Flatpicking Guitarists

Flatpicking Through The Holidays! - VHS Video with Booklet

Lead Breaks to Bluegrass Songs Flatpicking Style - Video

Flatpicking With Doc (and Steve) - DVD with Booklet

The Art Of Crosspicking - DVD with Booklet

Learn To Flatpick 1, 2, 3 - 3 DVD Set - Beginner, Intermediate and Advanced with Booklets

Easy Gospel Guitar - DVD with Booklet

Basic Bluegrass Rhythm Guitar - DVD with Booklet

4 Hr. Bluegrass Workout - Book with 4 CD

Flatpicking The Gospels for Mandolin Book w/CD - Audio

Kaufman's Favorite Fifty Celtic Hornpipes for Mandolin Book and CD

Kaufman's Favorite Fifty Celtic Jigs and Waltzes for Mandolin Book and CD

Kaufman's Favorite Fifty Celtic Reels A through L for Mandolin - Book and CD

Kaufman's Favorite Fifty Celtic Reels L through W for Mandolin - Book and CD

Blazing Mandolin Solos for One or More - Book with CD

Smokey Mountain Christmas For Mandolin - Book with CD

20 Bluegrass Mandolin Solos That Every Parking Lot Picker Should Know Vol. 1 Book with/ 6 CDs

20 Bluegrass Mandolin Solos That Every Parking Lot Picker Should Know Vol. 2 Book with/ 6 CDs

20 Bluegrass Guitar Solos That Every Parking Lot Picker Should Know Vol. 1 Book with/ 6 CDs

20 Bluegrass Guitar Solos That Every Parking Lot Picker Should Know Vol. 2 Book with/ 6 CDs

20 Bluegrass Guitar Solos That Every Parking Lot Picker Should Know Vol. 3 Book with/ 6 CDs

20 Bluegrass Guitar Solos That Every Parking Lot Picker Should Know Vol. 4 Book with/ 6 CDs

20 Swing Tunes Guitar Solos That Every Parking Lot Picker Should Know - Book with 6 CDs

20 Gospel Songs Every Parking Lot Picker Should Know - Book with 6 CDs

4 Hr. Bluegrass Workout for Banjo - Book with 4 CDs

Steve Kaufman's Listening Materials also at www.flatpik.com CDs * Videos * Cassettes * DVDs

Stylin' with guest Red Rector - CD

Back Home with 2 Time Flatpicking Champ Robert Shafer - CD

Circles - Solo Steve - CD

Star Of The County Down with Robin Kessinger - CD

Bullet Train - CD

The Arkansas Traveler - CD

To The Lady - CD

Breaking Out - CD

Frost On The Window - Cass. Only

Winfield Winners - 8 Champs in Concert! Live concert from Kamp - DVD

Steve Kaufman - *Flatpicking to the Next Level* - Live Show Video - DVD

Strange Company with Nancy Strange, Don Cassell & Will Byers - Cass. Only

An Evening With Steve Kaufman - Live Show Video - VHS Only

Doc's Guitar Jam - Recorded Live at Merlefest w/ Steve Kaufman, T. Rice, D. Crary and more - VHS or DVD

The Best Of The Camp Concert Series - Volume 1 and Volume 2 CDs - Live from 1998 and 1999

The Best Of the Kamp Concerts - Volume 3 - 2 CD set - LIVE from 2000

The Best Of the Kamp Concerts - Volume 4 - 2 CD set - LIVE from 2001

The Best Of the Kamp Concerts - Volume 5 - 2 CD set - LIVE from 2002

The Best Of the Kamp Concerts - Volume 6 - 2 CD set - LIVE from 2003

The Best Of the Kamp Concerts - Volume 7 - 2 CD set - LIVE from 2004

The Best Of the Kamp Concerts - Volume 8 - 2 CD set - LIVE from 200S

Some of Steve's Goodies

Steve Kaufman's Flatpicking Kamp Embroidered Denim Shirts

Steve Kaufman's Acoustic Kamp T-Shirts

Steve Kaufman's Acoustic Kamp Denim cap w/ Suede Bill

Kamp Kazzos, Water Bottles, Seat Cussions, Fly SwattersTote Bags and more

Steve's Strings - DR Handmade Strings MH .13-.56 or D'Addario Med J-17

Steve Kaufman's Yellow Picks - 10 to a Pack

To receive Steve's newsletter, catalog or tour schedule call
800-FLATPIK in North America
Outside the N. America +865-982-3808 voice / Fax
Steve Kaufman
PO Box 1020
Alcoa, TN 37701

Order on line and sign up for Steve's Email List at www.flatpik.com
Questions and Comments to: Steve@flatpik.com